THE RED SATIN SHOES

Melissa Saari

Whimsical Publications, LLC

Florida

The Red Satin Shoes is a work of fiction. Names, characters, and incidents are the products of the author's imagination and are either fictitious or are used fictitiously. Any resemblance to actual events or persons, living or dead, is entirely coincidental.

To purchase the authorized electronic edition of *The Red Satin Shoes*, visit www.whimsicalpublications.com

Cover art by Traci Markou
Editing by Janet Durbin

ISBN-13: 978-1-936167-89-0

Published by
Whimsical Publications, LLC
Florida

Acknowledgements

I would like to thank Janet Durbin and Whimsical Publications for their efforts to publish this book. I would also like to thank Southern New Hampshire University for giving me the writing skills and all the other skills writers need these days.

I'd also like to thank my tireless editor, Will Hardman, and my editor at Whimsical Publications, for polishing the writing. Editing a manuscript is difficult, but editors are like Michelangelo, bringing the angel's wings to life.

Patricia McDonald has been outstanding by supporting my own writing, since she's been an established writer for years, and many other authors have followed in her wake. They all deserve my congratulations and respect.

As Kim kept moving the flashlight, she caught sight of two bare feet poking out from behind a box. She could see them quite clearly: pale, translucent feet with well-kept nails; and she realized the intruder must be young. Kim was surprised to see a child down here in the basement.

The sound of crying slowly filtered into her awareness. Feeling compassion for the young person who must surely be lost, Kim walked forward, carefully avoiding the spilled milk and shattered glass.

She went around the boxes and shone her flashlight on the legs, noticing a lacy hem line on a linen dress as she ran her flashlight up the stranger's body.

Her hands were still shaking, but she continued to raise the light, inch by inch, uncovering every detail, fascinated by each discovery.

She drew in a breath sharply as the light finally revealed a young girl, about ten she guessed, cowering against the wall, with her head down.

The girl's outfit was an old-fashioned skirt with lace frills around the edge, and Kim remembered lace like that on her grandmother's table. Her grandmother had crocheted it herself: fine, crocheted circles and pineapples and shells.

"Are you all right?" she asked the girl.

The girl remained sitting with her head hung low, her mop of red hair obscuring her face. As Kim spoke to her, she began raising her head until her face came into view. Kim screamed in surprise.

Above the small, dark mouth, the eye sockets ran deep and empty, nothing but blackness behind them, the hollow recesses of the braincase echoing back at her.

Kim was struck hot with terror at the realization that she was looking at a ghost. She expected this kind of surprise would make her even colder than she was now, but it didn't.

Kim felt a strong surge of compassion and pity for this ghost before her. Even though her skin prickled in fear, the deep emotional connection she felt with the spirit overrode her body's reactions of horror and disgust. After all, hearing about a ghost, and seeing one, were two different things, really. She stood her ground, and then saw the dark mouth open and ask her a question which sent a chill through to her bones.

"Have you seen my red satin shoes?"

"You're dead!" Kim shouted. As the words rushed out her mouth, she felt more alive than she had in years.

"Have you seen my red satin shoes with the buckles?"

"What are you talking about?" Kim asked.

"Have you seen my red satin shoes?" the ghost inquired.

"I must be losing my mind," she said, although the ghost didn't even turn her head at the comment.

Kim closed her eyes tight and rubbed her fingers against them until beautiful colors formed. Even behind her closed eyelids, she could still feel the girl's presence.

"Have you seen my red satin shoes?" the eyeless ghost demanded.

Kim snapped her eyes open. She was still there, and the eye sockets were still empty dark holes. Kim finally comprehended the ghost wasn't a hallucination and wasn't going to go away just because she wished it or rubbed her eyes.

"I've never seen your red satin shoes!"

She wasn't sure if the ghost misunderstood her or was simply lost in her own purgatory. "So you have seen my shoes? I knew it, you lying thief! Give them back! Give them back! Give them back!"

With each repeated command, the ghost's voice grew fainter and fainter, as if it was being pulled farther and farther away from her. Then the ghost disappeared from sight entirely and the tension in the air eased to a more normal level, as if the ghost had never been there at all.

Dedication

This book is dedicated to my mother, Marge Clark, who has always been my inspiration, and one of the most avid readers I have ever met.

Chapter One

The wine fields of Sonoma County stretched on for hundreds of miles through the rolling hills and endless valleys of the Wine Country, but to Kim it looked like the endless graveyards for the victims of alcoholism that littered California.

Her family's mansion had once been shining white and spotless. Now, it was decaying with the land, as if the rotting vineyard outside had sent its venom through the dirt, flooding the house with age and destruction. The remaining paint on the walls was cracked and peeling and the fields of bricks in between were so old they had turned a deep brown.

Hanging overhead, huge thunderclouds pounded the earth with lightning and what felt like a month's worth of rain, and the lightning caused the raindrops to sparkle like crystals as they spattered against Kim's window. The moon glowed through the breaks between the clouds like a ghost escaping from inside.

Kim lay in her bed, watching the clouds roll by. She'd been watching the storms for thirteen years from the same room. She imagined faces in the bellies of the clouds, angry spirits, and she shivered.

The wind shrieked past the eaves of the house and shattered against the window. Kim watched the panes shake in the half-light of the storm flashes, as if the wind was trying to drag them away and pull her into the storm with the window.

The old heater rattled at the end of the bed. It gave her

comfort to have the familiar red power light emit a faint radiance to ward off the darkness and to have the warmth against her feet.

The window rattled again, louder this time, and the thunder sounded at almost the same moment the lightning flashed. Kim knew the storm was directly overhead.

"Oh, you haven't got the best of me yet, you old storm!" she whispered.

The air was crackling with pent-up energy and she could smell the scent of fresh ozone in the air. She felt the hair on the back of her neck stand straight up.

For a brief moment Kim forgot her fears and suddenly felt alive, inspired, excited, as if she was being lit up.

She sat up and looked out the window just as the lightning hit full force. The old oak tree illuminated in a blue-white glow when the lightning ripped through the branches. A side-bolt struck the metal Radio Flyer 76 wagon left in the yard and buried itself into the ground beneath the cart, making the very earth glow white with heat.

Yet another side-bolt arced across the lawn to the street nearby and buried itself in the power box on the pole, as if that had been the purpose of the power box all along, to absorb the energy from the angry skies.

At the same time, all the power went off in the area and blackness cloaked everything. To Kim, it was like the lightning had wanted to outshine every single light around and pulled it inside.

There was dead silence while the afterimage of the strike burned green in her vision. Then the thunder struck.

She watched the glass in the window bend inward from the blow instead of outward like they had before when the storm pulled at them, and her eardrums rang from the huge blast of sound. The pressure in her inner ears was so great she imagined she felt the pressure rise in her brain, causing her to cover her ears in fright. Then she heard a branch crash to the ground with a tremendous splintering, could hear it even through the ringing that still tolled in her ears.

Even though she had not been hit by the lightning directly, Kim still felt herself shaking uncontrollably. She was so shocked by the narrow miss; she felt everything leave her mind in a panic. She inhaled through her nose trying to calm herself down, and to see if she could smell any smoke. Kim smelled nothing but the rain and the ozone and nitrogen gas. She began to relax, not sensing any fire.

As the ringing faded, Kim tested her hearing, but all she heard was her own fingers rubbed together near her ears. The sound of her brother, James, belching and moaning slowly crept into earshot, and she knew he'd been drinking again. He always belched a lot when he was drinking. Then she heard him getting rid of the extra alcohol in the fastest way possible, same as he had in the past, by throwing up

"Too much to drink again, Jamie?" she asked, not because he could hear her up in her bedroom on the second floor, but more to relieve her tension and bring her back to reality.

She looked at her heater, and noticed the red light was no longer on. She realized the reason she couldn't hear anything else was because the power was still off. She had forgotten that detail in the shock of the moment. Kim felt the goose bumps, like an alien infestation, poking through her skin as she rubbed her hands across her arms, trying to warm herself up.

Kim remembered the fuse box in the basement that would need to be reset when the power came back on. Since the transformer down the street had been hit and the one in front of her house wasn't damaged, she hoped to get the power back on quickly.

Further down the street, she could already see other houses with their lights flickering back on, so it was worth a shot.

Kim saw her sweater hanging nearby on a chair with the next flash of lightning.

She shivered in the cold air. Once more the compressed air rippled against the window, making it rattle like a rattlesnake in the grass whenever Kim got too close.

"Now who's going to fix the fuse box?" she asked herself. "My brother's useless. Mom's out on a date in Sebastopol. And my father...well, there isn't any chance of him coming back, is there?" Kim's father had left when she was six, before she could form any vivid memories of him. "I guess it's up to me."

During the next lightning strike Kim noticed a flashlight

on her desk and memorized where it was. She went across the room in the dark, stopping when she felt the table on her legs, and found the flashlight by touch. A small circle of light shone before her, darting this way and that as she looked around.

Kim grabbed the dark blue knitted sweater off her wicker chair and exited the room.

Chapter Two

She inched her way downstairs, hanging onto the banister as she went, step by step. Knowing the staircase was unstable, she was very careful where she placed her foot and made it to the bottom safely. She turned the corner and shone the light in the direction of the bathroom. The door was wide open. She went over and looked inside, suspicious of what she would see.

Sure enough, the beam of the flashlight illuminated her brother's chest, his bony ribcage poking through the thin pajamas. James was fast asleep on the floor next to the toilet. The bathroom stank badly and Kim realized he must have fallen asleep before flushing.

"Useless," she muttered.

Braving the smell, she walked over to James, nudging him in the ribs with her slippers three times, but James didn't wake up. His ribs continued going up and down in the same slow motion they had before.

"Completely useless," said Kim, but even speaking directly above him, he didn't stir.

When she entered the rickety old room filled with dilapidated cabinets and what could pass for turn of the century appliances, her light shone on the equally old pots and pans. The light also illuminated the basement door. The light bounced off the kitchen window and reflected so bright she saw little purple dots in her vision and had to wait for her night vision to return before she could safely continue her journey to the basement door next to the bread cupboard. Grabbing a chunk of bread, Kim shoved it in her mouth then headed for the basement.

Kim hated the basement. For one thing, it was dark down there and her mother never cleaned it, so it smelled like years of dust and rot. For another thing, the water heater and furnace made such strange noises: banging and groaning and hissing. Usually when someone had to go into the basement, she could convince her older brother James to do it. But this time she was on her own.

Chills ran down her spine as she reached the basement door. Without the heater on, the doorknob was freezing.

She drew in a quick breath and yanked her hand away. "Oh man, that's cold! James, I hope you're happy! Next time I'm waking you up, even if it takes a whole bathtub of ice water!"

She found the courage to reach forward again.

Wrapping the arm of her blue sweater around her hand, she carefully opened the basement door. Kim's hands were shaking, and soon her frame was shivering, too.

She was shaking so bad the knob rattled with her shivering. The sound bothered her so she let go of the door and watched it start to close before pulling it open again. She stepped through and began going down the steps warily.

Clutching the railing like she was choking it with her fingers, she edged down towards the blackness filling the space below. Small things skittered across the floor and she had to hold back a screech. "Great," she said to herself. "Mice playing soccer."

Kim's imagination was running wild at what lay below, causing her to forget about the gap on the steps. Her ankle slipped through where the third step used to be before gravity began to drag her down. Teetering back and forth, Kim could only imagine what lay beneath her, waiting for her to tumble into their grasp.

She held on to the banister with one hand while the other pinwheeled to keep her from falling forward, knocking the flashlight out of her hand.

It bounced down the stairs until it landed at the bottom, resting against the last step so the light shone up the staircase enough for her to see.

Horrible visions loomed up at her from the darkness beneath the stairs: bones, faces, and the smell of the gas and mold she always associated with death. Only the edge of one shoe barely on the step and her death grip on the banister stopped her falling to meet them.

After she put both feet on firm flooring and her legs stopped shaking, she continued downstairs slowly, following the shadows cast by the steps as they interrupted the beam of light.

When she got to the bottom, she grabbed the flashlight and shot a bright ray of blue light around the room, warding off any evils that might be lurking in the darkness. Mice fled in front of the pale beam like little vampires escaping the rising sun.

"That's better," she said to herself, realizing her foolishness. "Now where's the fuse box?"

Chapter Three

Moving her flashlight around the basement, Kim finally saw the fuse box on the opposite wall at eye level. Keeping the light turned downward so she wouldn't trip over anything, she moved toward it.

Even though she illuminated the darkness, she still couldn't get her hands to stop shaking, leaving a wavering puddle of light on the floor. She held the handle with both hands, mentally telling herself to calm down.

She stopped, took a deep breath, and reminded herself what her mission was before carefully moving toward the fuse box again, this time not so shaky.

Chasing away an uncomfortable feeling, she reached out to touch the fuse box. Before her hand reached the cover, Kim heard a crashing sound behind her. She panicked, gasping in fear, and every monsters she had imagined before loomed to life in her mind. She drew her hand back quickly and spun around.

The first thing Kim noticed was a window partly open across the basement, high up the wall. She wondered if someone would break in here in the middle of a storm. Could the intruder be some transient? Could there be a homeless person looking for a place to stay warm? Sensible when she wasn't scared half to death, she couldn't imagine a serial killer walking around in a storm like this, and decided her first instinct was probably right, probably some homeless person looking for a way out of the storm and fell when he sneaked in through the window. It was a far better thought than a monster or a walking pile of bones.

Then she looked down at the floor and realized where the crashing sound actually came from.

A jug of milk had tumbled over onto the floor from a milk crate and the glass lay broken and flashing in the light. A white puddle was spreading across the floor like a Rorschach test.

"That's strange. Who would keep milk down here? The milk should be in the pantry."

As Kim kept moving the flashlight, she caught sight of two bare feet poking out from behind a box. She could see them quite clearly: pale, translucent feet with well-kept nails; and she realized the intruder must be young. Kim was surprised to see a child down here in the basement.

The sound of crying slowly filtered into her awareness. Feeling compassion for the young person who must surely be lost, Kim walked forward, carefully avoiding the spilled milk and shattered glass.

She went around the boxes and shone her flashlight on the legs, noticing a lacy hem line on a linen dress as she ran her flashlight up the stranger's body.

Her hands were still shaking, but she continued to raise the light, inch by inch, uncovering every detail, fascinated by each discovery.

She drew in a breath sharply as the light finally revealed a young girl, about ten she guessed, cowering against the wall, with her head down.

The girl's outfit was an old-fashioned skirt with lace frills around the edge, and Kim remembered lace like that on her grandmother's table. Her grandmother had crocheted it herself: fine, crocheted circles and pineapples and shells.

"Are you all right?" she asked the girl.

The girl remained sitting with her head hung low, her mop of red hair obscuring her face. As Kim spoke to her, she began raising her head until her face came into view. Kim screamed in surprise.

Above the small, dark mouth, the eye sockets ran deep and empty, nothing but blackness behind them, the hollow recesses of the braincase echoing back at her.

Kim was struck hot with terror at the realization that she was looking at a ghost. She expected this kind of surprise would make her even colder than she was now, but it didn't.

Kim felt a strong surge of compassion and pity for this ghost before her. Even though her skin prickled in fear, the deep emotional connection she felt with the spirit overrode her body's reactions of horror and disgust. After all, hearing about a ghost, and seeing one, were two different things, really. She stood her ground, and then saw the dark mouth open and ask her a question which sent a chill through to her bones.

"Have you seen my red satin shoes?"

"You're dead!" Kim shouted. As the words rushed out her mouth, she felt more alive than she had in years.

"Have you seen my red satin shoes with the buckles?"

"What are you talking about?" Kim asked.

"Have you seen my red satin shoes?" the ghost inquired.

"I must be losing my mind," she said, although the ghost didn't even turn her head at the comment.

Kim closed her eyes tight and rubbed her fingers against them until beautiful colors formed. Even behind her closed eyelids, she could still feel the girl's presence.

"Have you seen my red satin shoes?" the eyeless ghost demanded.

Kim snapped her eyes open. She was still there, and the eye sockets were still empty dark holes. Kim finally comprehended the ghost wasn't a hallucination and wasn't going to go away just because she wished it or rubbed her eyes.

"I've never seen your red satin shoes!"

She wasn't sure if the ghost misunderstood her or was simply lost in her own purgatory. "So you have seen my shoes? I knew it, you lying thief! Give them back! Give them back! Give them back!"

With each repeated command, the ghost's voice grew fainter and fainter, as if it was being pulled farther and farther away from her. Then the ghost disappeared from sight entirely and the tension in the air eased to a more normal level, as if the ghost had never been there at all.

Chapter
Four

Kim stayed rooted to the floor, too terrified to move, try-ing to rationalize what had just happened. She felt chills wash over her body and remembered the window was still open and knocking in the wind created by the passing thun-derstorm. She had completely forgotten about it when she saw the ghost.

She finished the trek to the open window without being bothered by any more apparitions, to her great relief. Once there, Kim closed the window, latching it to make sure it stayed shut. The rain rapped against the pane instead of coming into the basement, and the dripping sounds went away as the water cleared the windowsill.

The basement was now quieter than her ever-racing mind. Kim walked back to the other side, hoping there would be no more ghostly interruptions along the way. She sighed with relief when she made it and opened the fuse box then switched on the power. The old system thrummed to life. She breathed out a deeper sigh when the heater kicked on with a whoosh, pouring warm air through the basement, slowly warming her chilled bones. In the distance, she could hear thunder echoing, the worst of the storm past.

Once the light turned on with the returning power, the old fluorescent bulb sputtered to life over the course of sev-eral seconds, hiccupping its way into action. The basement was illuminated in sickening yellow hues. Through the hiccups of light, she noticed a rectangular shadow in the wall below the fuse box where two wooden strips had been torn away by a force she wasn't sure about, but thought it might have been from the surge hitting the fuse box. The light also illuminated a red square box on the floor not far away.

She noticed the top was ajar and moved closer to investigate, picking it up and studying it in the cold yellow light. The box was very old and made of wood, but she couldn't tell what kind because it was coated in bright red paint. She reasoned it must have fallen out of the newly opened secret hiding place, which is why she never saw it before. She noticed on one side something that looked like a date. She brushed the dust off carefully so she could read it more clearly. The name Charlotte shone through in white letters.

After studying the outside of the box, Kim carefully removed the lid. Inside, she found two perfectly preserved red satin shoes with gold buckles. She immediately recognized them as the shoes the ghost was asking about, the ghost she now understood was named Charlotte.

A single drop of something black clung to the buckle of one of the shoes. Kim carefully set down the lid to free up one hand and used her finger to brush it off. She was surprised to find it bone dry and flaking away from the gold buckle, though she shouldn't have been given the age of the box.

Staring at the object of the girl's desire, Kim felt a deep surge of guilt that she had no way to reunite the ghost with her shoes. But as she stood there with the box in her hands, she heard a whisper behind her.

"Save James,"

Kim got the creeps all over again when she heard the ghost's voice and looked around behind her, hoping at the same time that she would not see her. She was relieved to see no apparitions stood behind her.

Kim was confused by the message delivered from Charlotte because she didn't know how in the world she was going to save James, much less why she had to save him. He had been trapped in an alcoholic daze for years now, not even sobering up for social functions. The more he embarrassed himself, the less they were invited to social events.

Tired and cold, she made her way slowly and carefully back up the stairs. As she passed the bathroom on the way to her room, Kim noticed it was empty. James must have awakened and found some way to crawl back to bed. She quietly shut the bathroom door and crept upstairs to her room, trying to get to bed without James hearing her.

Chapter Five

The next morning, Kim woke up with the sun streaming through her windows. All the dark clouds from the day before had blown away during the night, taking with them any trace of the apparition. In the sunlight, the world looked less scary and more inviting.

Green grass and leaves coated with last night's rain glistened in the morning sun and turned the lawn of the house into a gleaming mirror. It was so bright she had to shade her eyes against the glare before she could see the branch from the oak tree resting in the yard.

Kim grimaced and muttered under her breath. The limb was longer than she was and five times as thick. It was embedded in the ground. There would be no way to remove it until the repairmen came out to repair the power to the other houses down the road. Then she knew they would notice the huge limb and remove it. She had seen the power company remove fallen trees before. Kim was very grateful to live in California, where the power company fixed damaged lines very quickly.

Luckily, the transformer for the farmhouse was still intact; its partner closer to the tree had absorbed the majority of the energy from the bolt, which was why the power came on when she reset the power box in the basement. She had been grateful for the heater last night, and had been able to sleep soundly when she managed to get warmed up, even after her scare with the ghost.

A hot bath is going to feel so good, she thought, flipping back the covers to her bed and swinging her legs over the edge. She looked at her bare feet on the floor and remembered the red satin shoes. The box with the shoes inside was resting next to her bed.

Downstairs, Kim heard her mother swearing and banging things around. She wondered why she was up at the same moment she realized it was Sunday morning. In a flash she understood what the ghost had been trying to tell her the night before.

"Oh, no!" she cried aloud. "It's Sunday! I've got to get ready for church!"

In much more of a rush now, she hurried to the bathroom, slipped out of her nightgown and waited for the water to get hot. As usual, the pipes poured cold water for a couple of minutes before they pushed hot water up to the second floor. She could hear them groaning and complaining like old ladies as they slowly churned the water up through their hollow insides. At last, the water began to run hot and she jumping in the claw-foot tub, her tired body relaxed for the few blissful minutes she had before her bath time was over.

Bloodshot eyes reflected back at her when she looked into the mirror while she combed her hair. She wasn't surprised at all because she'd been losing sleep for days. The sound of listening to her brother getting sick downstairs echoed in her memory. For the last three weeks now, James had come home smelling of alcohol, but it had gotten worse. Now, even when he was home, he would stay in his room and drink.

All night, James would take trips to the bathroom, belching and throwing up. During the day, he was bleary and angry. How in the world did anyone live a life like that? The more she thought about it, the angrier she became, and soon she was boiling.

Her strawberry-blonde hair was all wet and tangled and she spent several minutes avoiding getting dressed, pulling the hair this way and that with the brush until it looked more civilized.

After putting on her best church clothes, Kim pulled her hair back into a painful bun with a clip. She could hear the thumping getting even louder downstairs and knew Ellen, her mother, was almost ready to get them going. In the spur of a moment, she reached into the box and put on the red satin shoes she had found the night before.

The shoes felt cold, like a ghost had been holding them while they were in the box.

After the chill went away, they were very comfortable. Kim was surprised to find her feet fit inside the shoes perfectly.

For a moment, she felt like Cinderella and marveled at the coincidence that the young ghost in the basement had the exact same size feet.

"These were the little girl's shoes, weren't they?"

As if in response, the buckles twinkled brightly.

"Well, after all, church is where people go to be saved, isn't it?" she whispered, wondering if Charlotte would hear her.

"James, you lazy brat!" Her mother's angry knocking on his door downstairs echoed up the stairs. "Aren't you coming to church?"

Kim heard everything through the door where she stood carefully listening. She heard her mother's footsteps stomp across the floor and up the stairs. Kim wondered for a second if she was sober. Then she heard her mom stumble and crash against the steps. She stopped trying to climb up, breathing hard.

From the stumbling and gasping, Kim knew her mother had already been drinking that morning, before church of all things. She raged with frustration against her family, but kept silent as long as she could.

Even though she knew Kim could hear her just fine, Ellen yelled very loudly, her voice echoing up the stairwell like the voice of a fallen angel.

"Kim! It's time for church!"

"Okay, Mom! I'm getting ready! Geez!" Kim yelled back.

She listened to Ellen get impatient with James again after she had stumbled back down the stairs and made her way to his door. The knocking started again. "James! Are you coming to church or not?"

Kim could hear her brother's voice clearly. The house was so old that any insulation in the walls, if there had been any, was long since gone, chewed away by mice, leaving hollows in the walls that carried voices from one end of the house to the other. "Not today, Mom! I got the flu last night! I don't want to get everyone else sick."

Flu-schmoo, she thought to herself. *He's drunk again.*

Kim decided that since she was dressed and ready for church she could come out, so she stormed out her door and down the stairs to face Ellen, who was still standing in front of her brothers' room.

"He's a liar, Mom. Just an outright liar! Flu-Schmoo!" Her voice grew higher and higher with each accusation, and soon the walls were ringing with her fury. "James! Don't you know you shouldn't lie on Sunday?" The last word bounced down the hall and echoed into the kitchen before fading in the sudden quiet of the house.

James had no answer for her from inside his room. Ellen looked back at the stairs at Kim. She also had no answer, but wore a look of shock at her outburst.

Convinced she had gained the upper hand from her mother's silence, Kim erupted again. "What's the matter with him, Mom? Is he drunk again? What do you think?"

Ellen snapped. She drew in a very long breath, her face reddening, and screamed in an equally loud but far more threatening and dark voice, "Don't talk about your brother like that! He's got issues! He can't help himself!"

She slurped on her coffee, but the alcohol she had obviously poured into the cup must have burned in her throat because she started coughing, losing the opportunity to shout more for a few seconds.

As Ellen coughed on the coffee, Kim realized she had another chance to get her point across. "What are you doing, losing your sobriety before church? If Preacher Hardman saw you acting this way, do you think he'd invite you back next week?"

"You get ready for church, young lady, and mind your manners or I'll mind them for you!" Ellen walked back into the kitchen and slammed the door.

As Kim stared down the empty hallway, she muttered under her breath, "Need to stiffen up your drink, Mom?" before heading outside.

Chapter Six

Stepping outside, Kim noticed that the garden still hadn't been weeded, the porch was beginning to sag, and the upstairs windows were starting to get drafty as the wind and rain chipped away at the granite exterior. The only person who knew how to do that kind of work was James. But James was spending all his time getting drunk instead of taking care of the place, so the work wasn't being done.

As the minutes passed, Kim considered going to church alone. In the kitchen, she imagined Ellen pouring a little more vodka into the coffee, swirling it around, and drinking the rest of the cup. Then she would grab a throat spray from the counter and spray firmly three times into her mouth. After that she would breathe carefully against her hand, bringing it up to her nose quickly and checking the smell of her breath. Satisfied that no one could tell she had been drinking, she would quickly pour another cup of coffee and head toward the door. Kim had witnessed this action one too many times.

She wondered if she should tell her mom what she saw the night before in the basement but decided her mother would never believe her even if she did tell her.

She knew Ellen was ready to go from the chill she got down her back. Five seconds later, the front door slammed.

Ellen stopped at her side and looked at her carefully. "How come you always know when I'm ready to leave?"

"Because it gets colder every time you get closer to me.

It must be all that ice around your heart."

Ellen bristled at the sardonic insult, but knew that God, as well as the neighbors, could see her. "Watch your own heart, girl. Fire can burn out quicker than you think when the rains come."

"Let's go, Mom. And by the way, get rid of that coffee before you get to church. I can still smell the vodka even though you poured a fresh cup. Try rinsing the mug with vinegar next time."

"That was a very acidic joke! Let's go to church before you think of something else nasty to say."

Ellen took one last swig of coffee before dumping the mug and the rest of the contents carelessly by the fallen tree limb as she walked down toward the road to head toward the church with Kim.

The walk took Kim and Ellen past vineyards filled with buzzing bees that kept the grapes flourishing, so much happier than hers at home. Going past good vineyards while her family let their own land go to waste always hurt. It reminded her of the psalm they had to read in church about the fool that builds his house on a foundation of sand.

When mother and daughter reached the smaller houses on the edge of town, Kim at least felt better because then she didn't have to look at the vineyards. They walked down the sidewalk, close enough together to not have to tread on the grass, but still at a distance.

When they walked down past the graveyard to the church, Kim wondered if she would see any ghosts here. But the sun beat down so brightly the air practically glowed, and she hoped these souls were up in heaven instead.

Outside the church there was a sign announcing the hours of service for morning and afternoon. There was also room to write a nice saying every Sunday morning for passersby to ponder and enter into His service. To Kim, it seemed like a good way to keep people thinking about God even if they didn't walk into the church. Today the message read, "This house was built on a foundation of rock." A chill went down her spine as she recognized the same psalm she had been thinking about, wondering how she could possibly have known what Preacher Hardman would put on the sign this week.

The choir started singing before the rest of the church arrived to give everybody something uplifting to listen to while they showed up and got a seat before the main sermon began. They were singing "I Surrender All" when the pair walked into the church. Every time Kim heard that hymn, it always raised her spirits because she felt lighter than air when she gave all her worries away, surrendering all. It was one song that really got to her.

Because Ellen still believed her husband would return someday, she always had an empty seat for him at church. Even here, in the house of God, Kim felt alone, isolated on the other side of the empty cushion.

Preacher Hardman stood at the podium, an open Bible clutched in his hands. All of Kim's attention was on the preacher. Her mother had taught her good manners from a young age, before the alcohol changed everything, and she used them when necessary.

"I wanted to read to you today from the Book of Matthew, Chapter 9. This is the part about Jesus and the tax collectors."

Kim heard a general murmur run through the congregation, because she knew all the adults had to pay taxes or they would be in trouble. The preacher waited patiently for silence to return, which arrived quickly. He began his sermon by reading directly from the Bible, lowering his voice while reading Scripture to ensure that his voice resonated as deeply as possible, conveying the voice of a divine creature.

"And it came to pass, as Jesus sat at meat in the house, behold, many publicans and sinners came and sat down with him and his disciples."

Preacher Hardman paused for a moment to let that sink in. He raised his voice again to communicate with the congregation.

"Publicans were tax collectors hired by Rome from other nations. They were sent to do Caesar's dirty work because it was cheaper than hiring Romans. So basically they weren't very nice people. Look at modern-day tax collectors and you'll see what I mean."

Soft laughter rang throughout the congregation.

Father Hardman waited for silence.

"These people offended the Pharisees and everyone else

in the land by collecting taxes for a distant Roman emperor, and caused problems for many people as they collected the taxes. The Pharisees saw them sitting at dinner with Jesus and they were very confused. The next verse describes their confusion."

He lowered his voice to a deeper register to read the holy text. People all around her automatically dropped their eyes, following along in their Bibles.

"And when the Pharisees saw it, they said to his disciples, 'Why does your Master eat with publicans and sinners?'"

Preacher Hardman looked around the church, raising his voice to a conversational pitch again. "These Pharisees thought a Savior should sit with other religious people, the priests in the temples, rather than dinner with tax collectors at the other end of the spectrum. And it might seem confusing to you, too, but you need to hear what happened next. Let's read the next verses."

As the congregation's heads slumped back down to their Bibles, Kim kept her eyes on the preacher, his head down as he read the text himself. She already had the verse memorized. It was a popular story from the Bible, one that Kim had heard several times in church already.

"Jesus said, 'They that are whole need not a physician, but those who are sick. But go you and learn what that means, for I will have mercy, and not sacrifice; for I am not here to call the righteous, but the sinners for repentance.'"

Father Hardman took a deep breath as he prepared for the finale of the sermon. He had everyone's attention now. All eyes had returned to the preacher.

"I am not here to call the righteous to the Lord's service, but the sinners. How many here among us are sinners? Are we not called before God to be healed? If we are well and righteous, we already have God. And if we are sinners, all we have to do is let Jesus into our lives."

Father Hardman held his hands in prayer before his face as he bowed his head. "But O Lord, if there are any sinners, please let them be known. Give us a sign that they need your mercy!"

All was quiet in the church.

Kim felt something strange coming from her shoes, almost an itching. She looked down and saw the gold buckles in her red satin shoes were so hot her white socks had begun to burn, making her feet feel as though they were burning up with the increasing heat, sending thin tendrils of smoke past her knees. Immediately, horrified, she stood up.

She saw the other people crowded into the church notice the smell of the smoke and look around for the cause. It was pretty easy for them to find the source because the smoke was beginning to grow thicker and more pronounced as it came off her shoes.

They were looking in her direction and whispering to each other, then nudged their family members and pointed at her. Soon everybody was staring in her direction. Kim had never felt so humiliated in her life.

Then as the voices of the congregation rose, she heard what they were saying. The words stabbed through the air and hurt her ears, making them burn with embarrassment.

"Her shoes are on fire!"

"It's a sign from the Lord!"

In the midst of her embarrassment, she had forgotten that her feet were extremely hot, so she kicked the shoes off to stop the burning. They landed somewhere out of sight under the pew in front of her.

"Father Hardman!" she cried. The preacher looked up. Her mother tried to pull her down, but she held her ground. No longer the frightened girl in the basement, she stood proudly. "It's not about me! I'm not the sinner! The sinner is my brother, James!"

Before her mother could say anything, Father Hardman spoke directly to Kim, forcing Ellen to close her mouth in silence, embarrassment etched all over her face.

"I believe you, child." Father Hardman did not look angry at all. His expression seemed to reflect grace and contentment, a sort of fulfillment Kim guessed only holy people could feel.

Encouraged by the preacher's support, Kim continued, while her mother looked on in anguish.

"James is the one that's getting drunk all the time! He's the one who never helps out around the house! He didn't even show up here for church! This isn't fair! I'm not the sinner! He is! I'm scared for him, Father! He drinks so much that I think he's going to die. You have to help him. Last night he was so drunk I couldn't wake him up! Will you please help him?"

"I will, I promise," said Father Hardman. Then, quickly nodding in her direction, he took a step back and opened his arms wide to address the whole congregation.

"Once again the Good Lord has moved through our midst. Another poor creature may soon find the grace of the Lord, and it's all thanks to this brave lady."

Chapter Seven

Before the service ended, Kim made sure to carefully retrieve the shoes from under the pew. The buckles were still hot to the touch, but they were beginning to cool down. She carried them home, enjoying the cool grass on her feet.

Kim felt overwhelmed with happiness and good feelings, convinced the storm would pass and all would be well. Her mother, however, had other ideas. She was steaming mad on the way home from church and refused to say a word to her until they got home.

When they walked into the kitchen, Kim sat down at the table and kicked her bare feet back and forth, carefully touching the buckles again to see if they had finally cooled off all the way.

She watched Ellen gather stuff for sandwiches: bread, mayonnaise, and cheap processed meats. Nothing fancy like vegetables since no one took care of the garden anymore and they were too expensive. Just looking at the food made her depressed. . Kim watched her mother assemble the sandwiches with fervor, slapping the ingredients together as if snakes were fighting in her arms. Finally she slammed down the knife and splattered mayonnaise on the table.

"There, you happy now? See what you made me do! Ooh, sometimes you make me so mad!" When she said Ooh, her face twisted up into a half-horrified, half-enraged grimace. "What were you thinking, talking about your brother in church like that? Are you trying to get him in trouble?"

The last comment sent Kim spiraling into her own anger,

spouting back, "I'm just trying to help him!"

Her mother's face fell flat and threatening, completely unreadable, something Kim recognized as hazardous. Without any discernible emotion even in her voice, her mother dismissed her as coldly as a tyrant queen. "Get up to your room. I don't even want to see your face right now."

Kim knew her mother was dangerous in this state, but her own anger overwhelmed her and kept her from thinking straight. In frustration, Kim blurted out, "It would be my pleasure! I'm sick of watching you get drunk too!"

Ellen breathed in deeply and a very dark and angry look returned to her face. "I am still your mother! I will always be your mother! And you don't talk to me that way! You're grounded! I don't want to see you until tomorrow!"

"I'm starving! Can't I have some lunch first?" Knowing she was already in trouble, Kim couldn't help trying to get some lunch out of her mother.

"You can forget about that, young lady. You can think about it when you're upstairs! Get up there right now!"

Kim stormed upstairs, defeated, grabbing her shoes off her lap before she got up and noticing they were finally cool. As she got to the top of the stairs, she was so irritated she threw the shoes back down the stairwell, enjoying the knocking sound they made as they bounced. In her anger, she blamed the shoes for causing all the trouble in church, although something calm inside her mind assured her that she had done the right thing that morning.

Kim was already in her room by the time Ellen came over to the stairwell, curious to see what her daughter had thrown down the stairs. Ellen picked up the shoes, went over to the closet and placed them inside a shoebox. Then she thought about it for a few minutes as she sipped her whiskey and soda and reached a conclusion on how they came to be in Kim's possession.

Inspired by her idea, she decided to go upstairs with a sandwich to try and get more information out of Kim. Ellen decided that would definitely satisfy her curiosity and make her feel better.

After making the sandwich, she went upstairs to her room and carefully hid the red satin shoes deep inside the recess of her closet, one place she knew Kim would never dare to go.

Ellen didn't care if James entered her closet, though, as he probably would, searching for her booze. She only wanted to make sure Kim didn't find those shoes. Confident in her conclusions, Ellen walked over to Kim's room with the food, being careful to keep her steps even and measured.

Kim was inside her room eating some potato chips she had stashed away in case she got grounded again, which happened to her every couple weeks, when she heard her mother's footsteps before the knocking started. As soon as she opened the door, she regretted it because of the smell of whiskey on her mother's breath. She looked at the sandwich with happiness, though, and took it gratefully. Before she could get the door closed, her mother came in. She didn't see the bag of chips because Kim had already hidden it under her table, but she saw the shoebox in the corner immediately.

"About those shoes, we need to have a talk about them."

"You mean the red shoes I found in the basement?"

"Where did you say you got those shoes?" Ellen asked.

"Like I just said, from the basement."

"You stole those shoes, didn't you."

"No, of course I didn't."

Ellen pointed to the shoebox. "This box by your bed, where did you get that? Is that what the shoes came in?" Like a hawk, she swooped down and grabbed the box, reading the lettering on the side. "Charlotte? Is that who you stole them from?"

"No, Mom! Look how old the box is. Whoever owned those shoes is long gone." Kim was getting more exasperated the longer her mother interrogated her.

Her mother looked up with a gleam in her eyes that told of malice and hatred. "Oh I see. You're trying to be smart now. I still don't believe you, and you're still not getting the shoes back."

Kim was close to losing her patience entirely, and she began to plead with her mother to see reason. "No, Mom, you don't understand, I would never steal someone's shoes! That's ridiculous! You know I would never do something like that! I told you, I found them in the basement. They were in a hole in the wall and they popped out during the storm last night."

Her mother remained on the offensive. "That's the most outlandish story I've ever heard! Those are rock walls down there. If they are as old as you say, there's no way you could find anything down there that beautiful. The whole basement is full of junk. You stole them, didn't you? I didn't raise my daughter to be no thief!"

Ellen stood up, still holding the red shoebox, and turned to leave. Before exiting, she paused to add one last warning. "I'm taking this box away from you too, and keeping them both safe until you finally confess and tell me whom you stole the shoes from." She marched out of Kim's room, slamming the door behind her.

Kim quickly ate her sandwich because she was afraid her mother would change her mind and come back for it. After that, she finished her chips.

After eating, she sat down on the bed and stewed. She couldn't think of a single way to get through to her mother so she decided the best thing to do was try to find evidence in the basement. Kim opened her door silently and listened. She heard her mother closing drawers in her room, so she crept silently down the stairs and snuck into the basement, making sure to close the door behind her. Enough light shone from the ground-level windows that she could see her way down the staircase without falling this time.

She looked around all over the basement for evidence of what happened the night before, but couldn't find anything. It drove her mad with frustration. Kim searched for the dress the girl was wearing, even some of her lace, anything she could find to prove that she was telling the truth.

Searching through pile after pile, she dug her hands into the stuff trying to find anything to help her cause. A book of photos she had missed fell off a pile, landing on the ground with a thump. She picked up the ancient, dusty album. Inside, she found a picture of a little girl with the year 1910 and the name Charlotte written underneath in very faded ink.

Successful, Kim snuck back upstairs to her room.

Chapter Eight

Kim had just begun to look through the other pictures when she heard a knock on the front door. She put the photo album away quickly so it wouldn't be found. She heard Ellen go down the stairs and open the door and recognized the preacher's voice immediately.

"Good afternoon, Ellen. This is John. He is an interventionist."

Kim knew what was going on then. As she was heading downstairs to meet the interventionist, she heard Preacher Hardman asking Ellen, "Would you mind getting James? We really need to talk to him."

In the face of an interventionist and a man of the cloth, her mother said nothing as she left the room. In the ensuing silence, Kim walked into the living room.

"Hello, Kim. So glad you could join us as well. John, this is Kim, the girl who told me about James's problem."

"Then I'm very glad you're here, too," said John. "This is a small group. It's going to take all the love we have to make him better."

"Where three or more are gathered in my name," responded the preacher, quoting Scripture as usual.

Kim sat down on the chair by the sofa because it was softer to wait.

Ellen returned with James behind her, bleary-eyed and not completely willing. As Ellen led him to the sofa and sat down, James looked at the new person in the room in confusion.

Apprehensive, he looked at Ellen, pointing at John. "Who is this guy?"

"My name is John, and I'm here to help you though an intervention. I'm here because I was terribly addicted to speed quite a while ago, and then I got help. If I hadn't, I would not be here talking with you. The road that alcohol leads you down is not a good one, either. We need to talk to you today because it can't wait any longer, so I need you to listen to the people that love you."

Kim spoke first before her mother had a chance. "James, you were so drunk I couldn't even wake you up on Saturday night. You were passed out in the bathroom and I wasn't sure if you were going to be all right. You have to stop this getting drunk all the time! You need to get help."

"I can handle this on my own," said James, agitated.

Ellen decided it was time to say her piece, answering, "No, you can't handle this on your own. It's destroying you. I can't keep covering up for you. You're completely wasted, all the time, and you don't even come to church anymore! I need to you to be the big strong boy you used to be so you can help around the house. I don't want you making your little sister do all the work around here."

"Yes, but Mom, you need help too, maybe not as bad as James, but you drink too." Kim started up again.

Ellen sputtered. "How could you even say that? I wouldn't even drink if it weren't for James. I worry about him! I keep it under control."

Kim breathed in deeply, and breathed out again. She decided to keep silent.

The interventionist had something else to say at that point, keeping a very serious look on his face as he spoke to Ellen this time. "You know, we also have meetings at the Grange every Tuesday night. You wouldn't even have to talk a lot, just talk to us a little bit on Tuesdays. But James needs serious help."

Then John turned his attention back to James. "Since I've been in the room, James, you've almost fallen asleep twice, and you seem pretty confused. I'd say the alcohol is starting to take its toll on you. If you don't come in with us so we can help you, I don't know how much longer it will take before you end up in a hospital. I'd say, maybe a couple weeks. So what do you say, James? Will you accept our help?"

James remained silent, confused and agitated looks alternating across his face. Ellen spoke again, her voice barely above a whisper, "James, if you go, I'll start going to their meetings. I promise. I only want what's best for you, and the truth is what they say it is. The way you're drinking, you'll be in a hospital room before you know it. Just take the help, and you'll be better."

James stared directly at his mother, refusing to glance at the interventionist. Finally, after what felt like forever, he said, "For you, Mom, I'll go."

Ellen and James hugged each other, tears flowing down both their faces. After they separated, James left with John and Preacher Hardman, his head held high and his shoulders back in determination.

Once the front door was shut, Kim returned to her room and Ellen stayed downstairs. Hours later, she was sitting in bed reading "To Kill a Mockingbird" when Ellen came upstairs with dinner. She didn't even look at her mother. She was still upset about the accusation of stealing the red shoes. She hadn't even gone through the photo album yet because it felt so strange without James in the house. Even though he had spent most of his time in his room or out at the bars, she still missed his presence, even if there was a lot of groaning and belching involved.

Ellen didn't say anything when she set the tray of food down on the bed then sat down next to it. Encouraged by the silence, Kim began to eat the macaroni and cheese. After she had swallowed several bites, her mother found the nerve to break the silence.

"So I'll be going to those meetings on Tuesday like I promised. And James will get better. Everything's going to be okay, honey, all right?"

"Okay," she said. She figured it was easier to pretend to cooperate than to tell her mother how she really felt.

Her mother rose off the bed, straightened, then walked out the door and closed it behind her. Kim waited for her steps to go back downstairs before turning her attention back to the food left behind. By the time Ellen was downstairs, clinking the bottle against the wine glass, Kim had finished her dinner and gone back to reading her book.

Chapter Nine

Hours later, a loud crash downstairs surprised Kim out of her book, right when Atticus was about to shoot the rabid dog. She went downstairs to see what was going on.

When she reached the kitchen doorway, the first thing Kim saw was a broken bottle of what looked like gin soaking into the floorboards. Stepping inside, Kim noticed her mother passed out on the floor, breathing heavy but steadily.

The broken gin bottle lay close to her mother, the shards of glass scattered all around her. Kim knew if she walked on the shards she would cut up her feet too bad to walk. She stooped over, carefully picking up the broken bits piece by piece as she made her way across the room, leaving them on the counter out of the way.

By the time she reached her mother's side, a couple of small lines had been cut into her finger pads, large enough to allow the blood oozing up to form into little beads but too small to let them drip from her finger.

A chill went through her so she looked up from her mother and saw the ghost coming out of the wall towards them. Like one minute she was not there then the next her arms were slowly pushing through the wall and entering the room.

As the ghost crossed the floor, closing in on her and her mother, Kim started shaking her mother's sleeping form, crying, "Wake up! Wake up!"

"Have you seen my red satin shoes?" asked the ghost.

The ghost, Charlotte, was asking the same question as the night before. It made chills go up and down her spine all over again. She started shaking Ellen even harder.

"Mom! Mom! Mom, you really need to wake up!"

Ellen came out of her stupor long enough to say, "Uhhh."

The ghost repeated, "Have you seen my red satin shoes?"

Kim whimpered. Every time the ghost asked her question it was like a Chinese water torture, like needles tearing through her brain.

Her mother barely opened her eyes and mumbled, "What shoes?" Then her eyes closed again.

"Mom! Wake up! Wake up again! Can't you see the ghost?"

"I don't know what you're talking about, bothering your old mother about shoes and ghosts. There are no ghosts. Go back to bed."

Ellen's head folded down onto her chest in an alcohol in-duced unconsciousness. The way it fell reminded Kim of the way the ghost had her head tilted down last night. She tried to shake her mother awake again, but even the ghost's re-peated question could not wake her this time.

"Mom!" Kim screamed at the top of her lungs. She got nothing at all out of her mother this time.

Looking up at the ghost in anger, Kim yelled, "Why won't you just leave us alone!" The ghost answered with nothing, silence, not even her usual question. Only empty eye sockets stared back at her like two black wells.

Shrieking in frustration, and a little fear, Kim ran upstairs to her mother's room, knowing she kept a telephone up there for emergencies. She never bothered to put one down-stairs because she didn't want people disturbing her at mealtime.

Knowing Preacher Hardman's number by heart, she di-aled it and waited impatiently for him to pick up the buzzing line. While she waited, she noticed how much her hands were shaking, her fingers knocking into her temple as she cradled the earpiece to her head.

"Hello?"

"Preacher Hardman, it's me, Kim! There's a ghost in my house and she won't leave me alone!"

"Young lady, you should know better. There's no such thing as ghosts. All the spirits are up with God in Heaven or down in the pit of fire with the devil. Do you know what time it is? It's 2 in the morning. I can tell you're very upset. You just need to lie down and go to sleep and everything will be fine in the morning. Try not to call me so late at night next time, please."

There was a dial tone in her ear.

"Hello? Hello? Please? Oh no, oh no, oh no, oh no!"

As she gazed in horror across the room, the ghost came through the door, literally through the door, floating directly toward her.

"Have you seen my red satin shoes?"

In disbelief, Kim listened to the dial tone for another second, and then threw the phone down. The handset bounced, but she didn't watch to see where it landed because she was already running past the ghost, who turned slowly to follow her, and ran out the door.

She raced across to her room, slammed the door tight, and locked it just for her own mental security, even though her brain screamed, "That won't work!"

Kim dashed to her bed, shaking violently and utterly terrified. When the ghost came through the door without having to open it, she hid underneath the covers. Her mind completely panicked, shutting down and reducing her to a small dot in the universe. Even underneath the covers she heard the ghost's incessant question, "Have you seen my red satin shoes?"

No longer able to figure out any way to hide from the ghost that was tormenting her, the repeated question driving her out of her mind, she screamed at the top of her lungs, though only the ghost was listening.

"I threw your stupid shoes down the stairs! I haven't seen them since! Then my mom took the box away and blamed it all on me! Now why won't you just leave me alone?" Her voice got higher and louder the longer she screamed. Clasping her hands together, she screamed, "God, oh God, please make her go away! God, please make her go away! Make it stop, make it stop, make it stop, make it stop, make it stop!"

Curled up in a ball under the covers, Kim sobbed. After a

couple minutes of crying, the ghost had not repeated her incessant question. She stopped crying, wiped her eyes and listened. All around her she heard an infinite silence. Even the ticking of the heater and buzz of the lamp were gone.

Terrified, Kim pulled back the covers to see what lay beyond. Emerging from her cave, she saw no ghost, no blinding sun, and no strange apparitions at all. The ghost was nowhere to be seen.

Crawling out of bed, Kim carefully and silently opened the door to her room. She looked on the landing for the ghost. Charlotte was not there. She looked downstairs, where nothing had changed at all, but the ghost wasn't there either. She went back upstairs, convinced that the ghost was finally gone, that her prayers had been answered and that it would hopefully not bother her again. Kim was grateful for the nightmare to be over. She went back to her bed and closed her eyes. Within seconds her exhausted body collapsed into sleep.

Inside this sleep, Kim began to dream.

Chapter
Ten

Clifford looked down at his newspaper, riffling through the pages, and noticed that Japan had donated 3,020 cherry trees as a sign of peace between the two countries. As he read further, he noticed that Helen Taft had planted the tree for the White House. He spoke to his driver, Richard.

"1912 is not being a good year to the President."

Richard looked back at him with a grin on his face, one that Clifford could see through the large rearview mirror provided with the red Coupe de Ville, a new addition that allowed the driver to keep an eye on his passenger. His driver was especially proud of the innovative placement of the spare tire on the passenger door instead of the backseat door, because he was fond of the backseat and the spare tire kept the front door from opening as much as he'd like it to.

"Why is that?" asked Richard.

"He couldn't even find the time to plant a cherry tree from Japan. They'll be selling the cherries this summer to the tourists."

"Taft has got to be the laziest President we've ever had, Mr. O'Reilly."

"Indeed he is," Clifford agreed.

"We have arrived," Richard said, as they pulled up in front of the stately mansion that graced the wine fields of Sonoma County. The grapes glistened in the sun as he beheld the majesty of his estate. White paint covered every inch, without a single flake missing. It shone in the sun like redemption.

Clifford gathered the presents out of the backseat of the car and exited the vehicle, stepping onto his property after weeks of being on the road selling his wine.

Charlotte knew he was coming home the second she saw the bright red Coupe de Ville pull into the driveway. She ran down the stairs, past where her stepmother, Mary, was already waiting on the front porch. Her red ponytails bounced behind her, contrasting against her blue dress, as she ran to her father.

Nestor was weeding the garden, kneeling in the soft dirt, watching everything that was happening. "Have a care when you run that fast, young lady!" he cried out to Charlotte as she ran past.

Charlotte did not pay Nestor any mind, heading instead for his hugs. She knew when he had sold all his bottles of wine and had returned home once again, there would be more money and more presents and more hugs. This was something Clifford had done with her each and every time he came home.

He could tell she had been missing her father while he was away. When he went up to her stepmother first and presented her with a package, Charlotte's face twisted into a bitter grimace, showing she was jealous, but only for a moment.

"Why do you have to give her presents, Dad? She's not like Mom!" she asked him.

"It doesn't mean I love your mother any less, but we've moved on. Your mother's gone now. I have something here for you, too. I found it in a French store when I was on my business trip."

"French?" asked Charlotte. "I love French things!" The wooden box was delicately painted with flowers and a red background. It was tied with a light blue ribbon. She began to tear at the ribbon, wanting to get inside the box. That was when she noticed the ribbon was made of a flimsy material that fluttered to the grass in shreds as she tore it off the package.

Inside the box, Charlotte found a pair of red satin shoes with the gold buckles, still smelling faintly of the polish, that almost otherworldly polish that let Charlotte know beyond a shadow of a doubt that they were brand spanking new shoes of the finest quality.

"Oh Daddy, they're beautiful! How did you know I wanted these red shoes? They're so beautiful!" Charlotte beamed with joy and hugged her father.

Clifford returned the hug then looked at her with what he knew was a bemused look on his face.

"Go ahead, try them on!" He laughed at her enthusiasm and could tell it bolstered her confidence even more. She put the shoes on as quickly as she could without damaging them, relishing in the way the inside of the shoes slipped against her bare feet as she fit into them perfectly. She danced around on the front lawn with him, both of them laughing and grinning. It was a moment she and Clifford would treasure forever.

Their moment was interrupted by her stepmother's shrill complaint.

"Clifford O'Reilly, what are you doing spending all that time with her? I've been missing you too, you know! I'm your wife now."

"Oh come here, honey. I got you something else as well!"

Mary had already unwrapped the present handed to her earlier and was holding it in front of her gingerly, as if it were about to explode. "What is this thing? I have no idea what this black box is!"

"Honey, it's a radio!" He kept a smile on his face but he knew his eyes gave away his loss of joy. Charlotte had decided to go inside because things were getting rough again between him and her stepmother. Watching his daughter slowly go inside, he saw her shoulders fall as they continued to argue. Nestor was still weeding the garden, but he was pulling the weeds much slower than usual now. "What's a radio?" asked Mary.

"It's a box that voices come out of. That's how we can listen to the games on the East Coast and even listen to the news! These radios are selling like hotcakes in the city, babe."

"That's what I've got a newspaper for, you fool! You're the one who likes to catch up on the games. Did you get anything else?"

Clifford pulled a silver letter opener from his back pocket.

"This letter opener is almost 200 years old. It was crafted in Switzerland in 1719."

"Well, at least it's something I can use, but it's probably brand new, you rascal." she swatted him with the blunt side of the letter opener with an audible whack.

As Charlotte closed the door behind her, Clifford saw a look of happiness and sadness before the door obscured her face, and he was not sure how to handle it.

Chapter
Eleven

Time passed in the majestic house. It was a cold fall day with rain pouring when Charlotte left her room wearing her favorite blue cotton dress, listening to the rain hit the roof and the windows with its steady tapping.

The force of the taps created a rumbling sound that cut through Charlotte's awareness and reminded her of church bells with its serious, deep booming. The sound worked its way inside her head as she walked down the stairs.

She walked through the kitchen first, noticing the way the rain pounded with different tones as she moved through the house. She thought about her father who was gone on another business trip, but due back any day now. She heard a thumping as she passed into the drawing room. The sound was coming from directly above her.

She listened more carefully, and hidden deep beneath the rumbling rain was the moans of a man and a woman. Charlotte made her way back up the stairs quietly to investigate.

If her father was gone, who was upstairs, and why were they making so much noise? Her mind raced with questions.

Were they hurt?

Were they fighting?

She opened the door and saw her mother in bed, naked, as well as a man on top of her.

She screamed at the top of her lungs, afraid the man was hurting her mother. As he turned his head, a look of surprise etched on his face, she recognized Nestor.

"I'll tell Father!" she screamed, unable to contain her anger.

Mary must have realized her peril. She cried out, "No, Charlotte, stop!"

"I will, I will! As soon as he gets home I'm letting him know what you've been up to!"

She ran out of the room, crying because she was so furious. Before she left, she saw Mary jump out of the bed, as well as Nestor who dove behind the bed to get his clothes. Mary grabbed a gown and covered herself, then snatched up the silver letter opener and headed toward the door.

Charlotte had reached the top of the stairs when Mary caught her and pushed her from behind. For a second she felt fingers connect with her body, then the force of the push sent her tumbling down the stairs, her head landing on one step, her body bouncing and forcing her into a roll as she tumbled down the stairs sideways, then coming to a stop at the bottom.

Still grasping the letter opener, Mary quickly followed after Charlotte, noticing how she sat up, dazed, then in defiance. Furious and spiteful that she had not lain there longer, she descended upon her.

Before Charlotte could get to her feet, her mother quickly snatched her shoes off. The red satin shoes dangled out of reach of Charlotte's grabbing hands.

Charlotte screamed in rage. "I'll tell Father what you did!"

Mary glared at her. "If you ever want to see these shoes again, you're going to keep your mouth shut and do as I say, little girl. Your eyes are way too prying and get you into trouble."

Mary got angrier the more she thought about what was happening. Charlotte's smug face didn't help matters much either. In fact, it enraged her even more.

Charlotte screamed at the top of her lungs. "No! I hate you! Give them back! Give them back! Give them back!"

"You don't deserve them! In fact, you don't deserve to see at all!" she screamed. Mary raised the letter opener and stabbed it hard into Charlotte's eyes, back and forth, from one eye to the other, screaming between the thrusts, "Now, you'll, never, see, again! Now, you'll, never, see, again," over and over while Charlotte cried out in agony.

The letter opener, which Mary figured was about seven inches long, went deeper and deeper into Charlotte's eyes each time she stabbed her, and when it went in to where her hand was wrapped around the handle, Charlotte finally fell silent.

As the storm cleared from Mary's head, she looked down at her hand before pulling the letter opener slowly out of Charlotte's eye. All around her stepdaughter was blood: blood on the carpet, blood on her hands, blood around her eye sockets which were now black pits of emptiness.

She stared at the scene in front of her, taking it all in, processing it as if someone else had just done the deed.

Behind her, Nestor's voice snapped her out of her delirium, and she gasped. As Nestor spoke she came fully back to reality.

"Oh no, Mary, what are we going to do? She's dead!"

She continued to stare at Charlotte's body as if it would once again rise and swear vengeance. She didn't answer for many seconds, the rain pounding down outside. Mary scanned the surrounding area with her eyes, looking so see if anyone else might have crept in to witness her deed, terrified of being discovered.

After surveying her surroundings, Mary took one more look at Charlotte, and then back at Nestor. She said, "We need to hide the body. Somewhere they will never find her."

Chapter Twelve

Nestor knew if Mary looked at his face, she would see an extremely uncomfortable look. The way she had spoken about the poor little girl she had just slaughtered was like the way someone would talk about a bale of hay for some cow pasture far away, something you wouldn't care a thin dime about. This didn't seem like the way a woman should talk about her stepdaughter. But she didn't see the look, because she was still staring at Charlotte's body.

Wordlessly, Mary began to wrap the bloodstained carpet around Charlotte's body. When she was finished, he and Mary both lifted the rolled up carpet and carried it to the back of Nestor's Model T Ford that he'd been using around the vineyard and the garden. The back area was large enough to fit the carpet, her body, and a blanket to cover everything up.

They drove off into the dark night, silent, the rain pouring down so bad Nestor had to lean out the side to see his way through the trees.

The dirt road they drove on into the forest was far away from other people, other lights, and other witnesses. As they drove, Mary started to talk.

"We need to have a ransom note. We'll say that someone kidnapped her, then this ransom note will appear in the house somewhere. I'll figure that out later. Or, no, wait, in the mailbox, which would be a lot safer. It needs to say these kidnappers from Brazil want their money right away. Then he'll give the money to their man on the side of the street, and he gives the money to us, because he'll be working for us the whole time. Then we'll take the money and get out of here, far away from here, and we'll never have to think about this again."

"How are we going to pretend that she's alive?" Nestor asked. "We're going to need something to show him that the kidnappers are serious."

"I don't know. Let me think about it."

They continued to drive through the dark night with the awful load in the back.

"I know! Those red satin shoes back there in the house. I could tell him I tried to save her, but she lost her shoes in the fight with the kidnappers and now that's all I have left of her. That will convince him."

Seconds later she blurted out, "What about the letter opener? It's got her blood all over it."

"Relax, Mary," he answered in a calm voice. "I know what to do about that. It's not very big. I was able to hide it in my jacket while you were wrapping up Char-"

"Don't say her name!"

"The body. I know lots of places to hide something like that. The authorities will never find it."

"They'd better not find it, because if they try to blame me for this, I'm putting all the blame on you, so you better make sure they never find that letter opener, you got it?"

Nestor answered, "I've worked on farms all my life, raising baby animals, killing the old ones; the cycle never ends. Of all the farms I've worked on, I've never seen dirt as soft and rich as this dirt right here in the wine fields and the golden hills. You could bury something as deep as you want and it wouldn't even be a struggle to dig that deep, especially in this pouring rain. Nobody will find it for five hundred years until Mother Nature pushes it out of all that soft, earth. By then, even your great, great grandchildren will be gone and forgotten. They will never know the truth. I promise you this."

Although Mary breathed a sigh of relief, she continued to worry. "He'll pay the ransom," she said to herself.

"Are you sure?"

"Of course he will! He has to! He loves his precious girl so much he'd do anything to see her again."

As the Model T crept slowly through the trees, Nestor listened and heard nothing but the rain on the truck and the rattle of the engine. He let his foot off the gas and the truck ground to a halt in the mud. Before he shut the headlights off, he looked in front of the car and saw two great oak trees with a third one further back.

Once the lights were off, he and Mary found themselves engulfed in utter darkness. The clouds were so thick even the lights of nearby Sebastopol were gone, cloaked by the rain.

Confident nobody could see them, Nestor turned the headlights on again. "This is the perfect place to bury her body."

"Well, get to work!" said Mary. "I can't mess up my hands or Clifford will notice."

Nestor grabbed the shovel out of the back of the truck without a word and started digging a deep hole between the three trees, the headlights lighting up the site. The pounding rain never let up while he dug. The mud sloshed off his shovel as fast as he could lift it out of the ground, making the going slow.

Once the hole was dug, he crawled out of it, lifted the carpet and the body out of the truck, carried it over to the hole, and dropped it inside, exhausted.

He trudged over to the truck, covered in mud.

"Anything you want to say before we cover her up?"

Mary stopped smoking her cigarette long enough to hiss at Nestor. "What is there to say? It's pouring rain and I don't want to get wet. Besides, she's dead, so she's not going to hear me, is she? Just put a big rock on her so she doesn't wash away!" Then she immediately resumed puffing her cigarette, turning her gaze away from Nestor.

He obligingly lifted a heavy rock from nearby and dropped it in the hole. Then he began the grueling job of returning the dirt to where it came from. Once it was filled, he put an old pair of pruning shears on top of the ground because he didn't want to leave her in an unmarked grave.

Then, thinking twice, Nestor covered the shears up with more dirt and found the grass nearby that was turned upside down by the digging. He placed the sod over the dirt, hiding it forever.

The pouring rain had washed most of the mud off his clothes by the time he got back in the truck and headed away from the hidden grave.

After they had returned and changed their clothes, he and Mary hastily wrote the ransom note from letters torn out of the newspaper. By then it was morning, so he went to town to retrieve a matching carpet to replace the blood-stained one they had removed last night.

While he was gone, she was going to try to remove the bloodstains from her hands, but he knew it would be difficult work. She was furious at how hard blood was to get rid of by the time he got back. She had tried every cleaner she could think of in the house, and with a lot of work she was finally able to get her hands clean.

She retrieved the red satin shoes, put them back in the box, closed the lid, and walked down to the basement. She had decided to hide these as well, rather than use them as evidence. She informed him she had a better plan in mind already.

Mary carefully selected a wall in the basement where she knew it was already hollow. She opened it by pulling the nails out with a hammer. One of them popped out unexpectedly, giving her a knock on the shoulder with the hammer. She knew she would blame that on the kidnappers, as well.

She stuck the box inside, and tried to hammer everything back into place. The box fit snugly behind the wall, too snug-ly in fact, and she had to hit the last nail very hard to get the box to slide into place. Victorious, she went back upstairs.

When they returned upstairs, Nestor placed the new car-pet in the same spot the bloodstained one had been.

"The letter opener?" she asked. She was out of breath but still cautious.

"Completely gone. It will never reappear."

"Then everything is set," Mary said.

Nestor went back outside to work in an area of the gar-den hidden from sight, but where he could see what was go-ing on. No sooner had he reached it than Clifford's Coupe de Ville, bright red and shiny, pulled up in the front yard.

"Charlotte?" cried Clifford. "Where are you? You always come running out first! Charlotte?"

As soon as Mary heard Clifford's voice, she ran outside,

hysterical, and screaming, "Clifford! They took Charlotte!"

Clifford grabbed Mary as she ran towards him. "What happened? What are you talking about? Why didn't you call the police?"

"I tried to fight them, but they beat me up and said they would kill me if I called the police. I couldn't say anything. I was so scared. And then this letter showed up in the mailbox!"

Mary buried her face in Clifford's chest, crying, as Clifford grabbed the ransom note. He began yelling in rage.

"They could be hundreds of miles away by now!"

He pulled out of her arms and ran inside the house, and Nestor heard him shouting at the police on the other end of the line. Mary collapsed on the ground, praying and sobbing at the same time. It wasn't long before the police arrived from Sebastopol to ask all their questions.

As the police cars pulled up on the front lawn, Kim woke from her dream with a start, sitting up in bed in an ice cold sweat, wide-eyed and completely awake.

Chapter Thirteen

Realizing she'd fallen asleep in her clothes, Kim wasted no time getting up and running out of the house. Outside, she walked around the front yard until she discovered the object of her search already lay on the ground.

Underneath the limb of the huge oak tree, something glimmered and drew her attention there. Kim noticed the dirt had been plowed aside by the fallen limb, exposing the object. Pulling the sharp, tarnished object out of the ground, it took a little cleaning for her to determine that it was a very old letter opener.

Feeling confident in the reality of her dream now that she had found the murder weapon, she quickly got on her bike and took off down the road. Before long she came to the grove of three oak trees she remembered from her dream.

Kim marveled that nobody had cut them down. The proud trees stood in the middle of an alfalfa field, probably left there by some respectful farmer who chose to grow his alfalfa around them. It took her very little time to make her way through the field and reach the shade of the oaks.

Underneath the oaks, Kim started digging through the soil and discovered it was extremely soft. It separated beneath her fingers and disappeared in great piles as she cleared the dirt from the middle of the grove. Before much was gone, she felt a sharp prick on her finger and stopped. She carefully probed around and pulled out a pair of garden shears, also just like she had seen in her dream, but now extremely rusted from being in the ground for so long.

She picked up Nestor's ancient shears and put them in her pack.

When she got back home, Kim went upstairs without talking to Ellen at all. She was in the living room folding clothes anyway, so she decided it was better not to bother her until she had all the evidence she needed.

Upstairs, Kim opened the photo album again. This time she found a picture of Charlotte. Even though she had never seen the picture before, she knew from her dream the young girl was Charlotte, beyond a shadow of a doubt. It was an old black and white photo, the kind where the person had to sit still for a long time to take it. In the background, Kim saw the vineyard, but she did not pay it any attention because her focus was riveted on the young girl's face.

Kim closed the album slowly, making sure to leave a scrap of paper where the photo was hidden.

She went back downstairs and this time Ellen was paying attention to her because she was done folding the laundry.

"Kim, I'm sorry I didn't believe you. When I woke up I started going through the family letters. I found out there was someone called Charlotte that lived here a long time ago."

"Mom, everything is different now. I have a photo album with her picture inside, and I found some other things, too!"

Ellen came over to look and stared very carefully at the object in her arms. "That's the missing photo album! We've been looking for that for generations! Where did you find it?"

"Look who's inside, Mom!" Kim opened it to the page with Charlotte.

"That's Charlotte? Are you certain? I still don't know how you learned so much about her."

"I'm sure. I even know where she's buried, Mom. I found her grave. It's not far away."

"What!" Shock flew across her mother's face. She recovered quickly then yelled, "Well, let's go!" She grabbed her hand and dragged her to the car. Kim ran behind her, trying to keep up.

Ellen drove the car to the field, with Kim giving her directions.

She led her mother to the grove of oak trees, pulling the

shears out and showing her where they had left their mark in the earth.

Ellen didn't have anything as big as a shovel in the car, but she had a garden trowel in the trunk. Kim knew she kept it there in case James ever decided he wanted to do some garden work.

Her mother dug deep into the soil, and soon she had to stop. She tugged on something in the hole. Ellen lifted the fabric out and into the sunlight beyond the trees. Kim stood close to her, looking carefully as the first evidence was brought to light. The color had faded from the cotton from years of being in the damp ground, but a faint hint of blue could still be seen as the sunlight struck it.

"That's Charlotte's dress! You found Charlotte! Come on!"

Chapter Fourteen

Ellen grabbed Kim's hand again and led her to the car, but this time Kim was moving just as fast as her mother. Try as she might, she couldn't escape the feeling that a little girl was watching her from the other side. She could feel the sense of being watched fade as they drove toward town. Within minutes of crossing the town limits, Ellen screeched to a stop in front of the police station.

By the time she got out of the car and headed behind her mother, Ellen was already far ahead of her. The door swung shut before she could even get there. Kim opened it and went inside quickly, but by that time her mother was already talking, well crying really, to the woman officer at the front desk.

The officer, Kelly, from the name plate, looked unprepared to deal with the woman standing in front of her. Her eyes got quite large before Ellen even formed four words through the hysterics.

"There's a girl buried in the field by Bainard Road! You've got to come now! She's been there for almost a hundred years!"

The officer quickly recovered when Ellen finished her statement and immediately waved one of the other officers over.

The new officer, an older man who had a much stronger presence about him, spoke to Kelly quietly and calmly.

Where Kim stood by the door, she heard only the sobs as Ellen cried out "Charlotte O'Reilly." She could not make out the words of the officer as he comforted her. Other employees of the department started coming over and comforting her, too. This surprised her because she thought for sure they would think her mother was crazy. Instead, they appeared to taking her plea serious.

Then the older officer whose badge said "Hendricksonne" and some of his partners walked past Kim and out to their police cars. She wasn't sure how to pronounce the name so she didn't address him. Ellen was escorted to the older officer's car. Her mother looked so heartbroken about the body that Kim no longer felt embarrassed by her behavior. She began to feel sympathy for her instead.

That was when she realized the old anger she always felt between the two of them was going away. Before she had time to think about it, she was escorted to one of the other cars. The engines started and they were on their way down the road.

Deep beneath the three grand trees, the police uncovered a heavy rock, the tattered remnants of the carpet, and finally the remains of Charlotte O'Reilly.

When they were finished, a feeling of sadness washed over the onlookers. Once she was uncovered, the police began photographing everything. Then two of them got into the grave and began processing the scene for the evidence room.

Chapter Fifteen

That Saturday, there was a proper burial held at the family plot. Many people came from town to witness the funeral, people who had heard the story of the girl missing for almost a hundred years. Charlotte was in a marvelous casket, shining through the grim scene like a beacon. Kim had the red satin shoes clutched tightly against her chest.

When it was her turn, Kim walked up to the skeletal remains lying in the open casket. She felt sad that this was the last memory most would have of young Charlotte, then she placed the shoes gently between the bony hands, making sure the heels rested on the ribs. That way the young girl could have her red satin shoes with her for all eternity.

Looking up when she sensed someone watching her, she saw Charlotte, clear as day, standing at the end of the casket. She was smiling and her eyes had been restored to their vibrant blue color. She nodded once, peacefully, at Kim. Kim stayed rooted to the spot, too stunned to react.

Behind Charlotte, a light began to emerge, a light that hid the trees and sky behind her. From that light, a figure emerged. She recognized him as the girl's father from her visions in the dream. She watched, transfixed, as Clifford floated closer.

Charlotte seemed to understand as well, because she turned around and looked behind her toward the light. As she realized who was there, she spread her arms in welcome. The spirit of Clifford wrapped his arms around the young girl in a big hug, something she had been deprived of for decades. Kim could see the sparkling buckles on the red shoes covering Charlotte's feet as she hugged her father. Then the two spirits ascended into the sky, into the light, and passed from view as the glow flickered then faded away.

After the pair faded, Kim stepped away from the casket, tears of joy covering her cheeks, and went back home, carrying a feeling of peace, a peace that, for Kim, would never fade.

About the Author

Melissa Saari lives in Washington State where the Columbia River, the river that powers America, rushes near her front door, and every summer, smoke from forest fires fill the sky. These powerful elements inspire her writing, whether it's romance, fantasy, or horror.

Melissa also has two loving, protective dogs: a female pit bull named Marla and a male Chow called Leo. Her dogs provide comedy, therapy, and inspiration for her stories.

Melissa will always be a writer. She begins her Master's Degree in Screenwriting this fall to study the complex film industry and how her vision can be shared with billions of moviegoers.

www.ingramcontent.com/pod-product-compliance
Lightning Source LLC
Chambersburg PA
CBHW020600130626
46552CB00007B/2976